It's Mine, Christopher Bear!

STEPHANIE JEFFS
ILLUSTRATED BY JACQUI T

W9-BIQ-024

Everywhere Joe went,
Christopher Bear went, too.
He was Joe's best friend.
One day, when Joe was at preschool,
Oliver reached up to hold him.
"He's mine!" said Joe, grabbing Christopher
Bear. He pushed Oliver out of the way.

Harry was building a tower with the bricks.
Joe sat down next to Harry.
He gave Christopher Bear a brick to hold.
Then he started to build a tower, too.
"*I'm* playing with the bricks," said
Harry, knocking down Joe's tower.

Elizabeth was making a road.
She snapped the pieces together
and ran a bright green, shiny car
along it.
"Vroom! Vroom!" she said.
The green car slid off the track.
Joe picked it up.
"It's mine!" said Elizabeth.
"You can have this one."
She gave Joe the battered yellow car
with three wheels.

Jessie was busy at the paint table.
Jessie had the blue paint.
She stirred her brush
'round and 'round.
She sloshed the blue over her paper.
"I need the blue," she said to Joe.
"I'm painting a river."

Ben was cutting and pasting.
He had a huge, shiny catalog.
He flipped through the pages.
"I'm making a shop,"
he said to Joe.
"It's the biggest shop
in the world,
so I need all the pictures."

Joe and Christopher Bear went to play farmer.
Joe drove the tractor. Christopher Bear sat
in the trailer.

"I'm taking this bear shopping," said Oliver,
scooping up Christopher Bear.

"No, you're not!" shouted Joe.

He got off the tractor and grabbed Christopher Bear.
"You're not going shopping.
That's Christopher Bear—and he's MINE!"

"Mine, mine, mine!" said Miss Rosie.
"That's all I've heard this morning.
Harry doesn't want anyone else
to play with the bricks.
Elizabeth has made a lovely road,
but it's only got one car on it.
Jessie's used up all the blue paint
for her beautiful river.
And Ben has chosen all the best pictures for his shop.
And now Oliver and Joe both want Christopher Bear.
Whatever shall we do?"

"I know!" said Miss Rosie.
"Harry's bricks can make a bridge
for Elizabeth's road to cross Jessie's river.
And Oliver and Joe can take Christopher Bear
to Ben's shop."
Before long, everyone was busy.
Joe and Oliver chose lots of things
for Christopher Bear from Ben's shop.

Harry and Jessie helped Elizabeth build a bridge across the river. Then Joe and Oliver and Christopher Bear took turns at driving over the bridge. Christopher Bear nearly fell in the river, but Oliver saved him.

At story time they went to sit on the mat.
The story was all about friends.
Christopher Bear sat on Oliver's knee

next to Ben and Jessie.

"If you share your toys," said Miss Rosie at the end,
"everybody can be happy."

Then it was time to go home.

Oliver gave Christopher Bear back to Joe.

"That looks fun," said Mom.
She was looking at the road
with the bridge over the river.
"It is!" said Joe. He didn't want to go home.
"See you tomorrow!" he said to his friends.

At home, Joe helped Mom make some cakes.
Christopher Bear helped, too.
"When they're ready, you can share your cake
with Christopher Bear," said Mom.
"We shared our toys at preschool today," said Joe.
"Miss Rosie says sharing makes
everybody happy."

Joe shared his cake with Christopher Bear.
"We like sharing," said Joe.
"God likes sharing, too," said Mom.
"And he wants us to share with each other.
It shows other people we love them.
Sharing does make people happy!"
"It makes Christopher Bear happy, too," said Joe.
And Christopher Bear just smiled
his crooked smile made of button thread.

Large-quantity purchases or custom editions of this book are available at a discount from the publisher. For more information, contact the sales department at Augsburg Fortress, Publishers, 1-800-328-4648, or write to: Sales Director, Augsburg Fortress, Publishers, P.O. Box 1209, Minneapolis, MN 55440-1209.

First Augsburg Books edition. Originally published as *It's Mine, Christopher Bear!* copyright © 2002 AD Publishing Services Ltd. 1 Churchgates, The Wilderness, Berkhamsted, Herts HP4 2UB

ISBN 0-8066-4400-1
AF 9-4400
First edition 2002

02   03   04   05   06   1   2   3   4   5   6   7   8   9   10